A Follett JUST Beginning-To-Read Book

FUN DAYS

Margaret Hillert

Illustrated by Joe Rogers

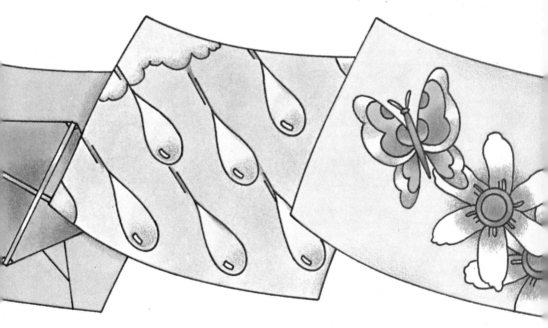

FOLLETT PUBLISHING COMPANY
Chicago

Library of Congress Cataloging in Publication Data

Hillert, Margaret.
  Fun days.

  (Follett just beginning-to-read books)
  SUMMARY: Describes in verse the celebration of a
variety of events and holidays.
  [1. Holidays—Fiction. 2. Stories in rhyme]
I. Rogers, Joe. II. Title.
PZ8.3.H554Fu [E] 80–21419
ISBN 0–695–41546–8 (lib. bdg.)
ISBN 0–695–31546–3 (pbk.)

Fifth Printing

I like this day.
I can have fun.
I like to play.
I run, run, run.

And this day, too.
Look what I do.
I jump, jump, jump
And you can, too.

6

Look up. Oh, oh.
Look at it go.
Up, up, and away.
What a good day!

7

On a day like this
See what I do.

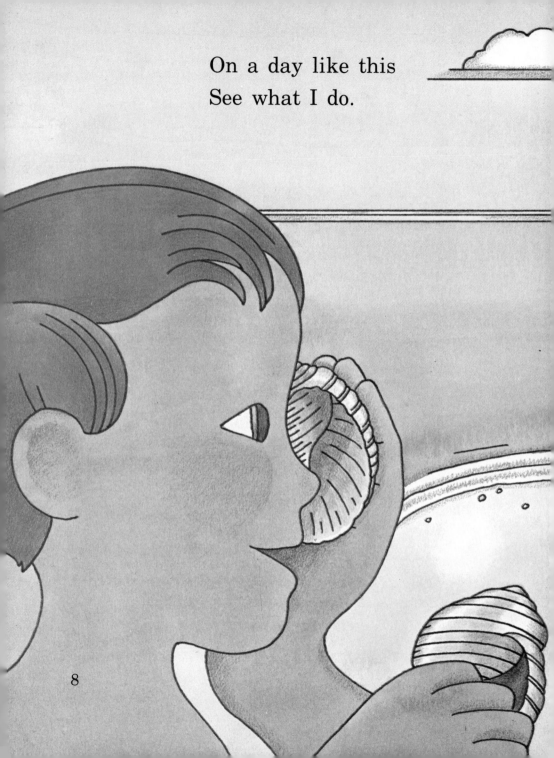

8

I like it here.
Do you? Do you?

Down, down, down.
Something comes down.

10

Red and yellow.
Yellow and brown.

11

What a good day
For us to play.
Can we make a man?
We can. We can.

Red ones. Red ones.
One, two, three.

What a good day
For you and me.

Look at us now.
Oh, me. Oh, my.

14

Something is green.
Can you guess why?

Something to play with,
Something to see,
Something to eat
For me, me, me.

16

This is the day
For Mother. Oh, yes.
And something for Mother.
What is it? You guess.

Come on. Come on
To see the fun.
Come on. Come on now.
Run, run, run.

This is the day
For Father. And look!
Something for Father,
A Father's Day book.

How pretty! How pretty!
Up, up, and away.

20

I like it. I like it.
Oh, what a good day!

21

What day is this?
Can you guess, guess, guess?
A day for school.
Oh, yes. Oh, yes.

Look, look, look.
What fun! What fun!
Look and see
This funny one.

We go in the car.

Now guess where we are.

24

We get out and run.
Oh, this is fun.

We eat and we play.
We eat and we play.
We EAT and we PLAY . . .
I like this day!

Something is big
And pretty to see.
Something is here
For you and for me.

Something to eat
And something for play.
What fun it is.
And what a good day.

Guess what this is.
What do you see?
This is my day,
A big day for me.

I like it. I like it.
This is the one.

I want you to help me.
Come help with the fun.

Margaret Hillert, author of many Follett JUST Beginning-To-Read Books, has been a first-grade teacher in Royal Oak, Michigan, since 1948.

Fun Days uses the 69 words listed below.

a	get	make	school
and	go	man	see
are	good	me	something
at	green	Mother	
away	guess	my	the
			this
big	have	now	three
book	help		to
brown	here	oh	too
	how	on	two
can		one(s)	
car	I	out	up
come(s)	in		us
	is	play	
day	it	pretty	want
do			we
down	jump	red	what
		run	where
eat	like		why
	look		with
Father			
for			yellow
fun			yes
funny			you